D0636325

Some of
My Best Friends
Are Monsters

Some of My Best Friends Are Monsters

by

Bruce Coville

Illustrated by
Tom Newsom

A GLC Book

A MINSTREL® BOOK

PUBLISHED BY POCKET BOOKS

New York   London   Toronto   Sydney   Tokyo   Singapore

**For Curtis,
son of Robert**

This book is a presentation of Newfield Publications, Inc. Newfield Publications offers book clubs for children from preschool through high school. For further information write to: **Newfield Publications, Inc.,** 4343 Equity Drive, Columbus, Ohio 43228.

Published by arrangement with Pocket Books, a division of Simon & Schuster Inc. Newfield Publications is a federally registered trademark of Newfield Publications, Inc. Weekly Reader is a federally registered trademark of Weekly Reader Corporation.

A MINSTREL PAPERBACK *ORIGINAL*

 A Minstrel Book published by
POCKET BOOKS, a division of Simon & Schuster Inc.
1230 Avenue of the Americas, New York, NY 10020

Copyright © 1988 by General Licensing Company, Inc.
Cover artwork copyright © 1988 by General Licensing Company, Inc.

Special thanks to Pat MacDonald, Robin Stevenson, and Gwendolyn Smith.

Cover art and illustrations by Tom Newsom
Book design by Alex Jay/Studio J

ISBN: 0-671-64747-4

First Minstrel Books Printing August 1988

A MINSTREL BOOK and colophon are registered trademarks of Simon & Schuster Inc.

"Camp Haunted Hills" is a trademark of General Licensing Company, Inc.

Printed in the U.S.A.

Chapter One

Harry Goes Berserk

Do you know what rice pudding feels like when it slides down your back? I'm no big fan of the stuff, anyway. (I mean, think about it. What does rice pudding look like to *you*?) But I can tell you this much: I'd rather eat it than wear it. So when Lucius Colton dumped a bowl of it down my T-shirt during our fifth week at Camp Haunted Hills, I was not amused.

This was not true of the rest of the kids at my table. They all seemed to find it incredibly funny. Eddie Mayhew laughed so hard that milk came out his nose.

I suppose I might have laughed, too, if it had happened to someone else. But Lucius had chosen me to be the main victim of his warped personality, and I was getting pretty tired of it.

I had already talked to our counselor, Dan Snopes, about the problem. He suggested that maybe Lucius was jealous because I had turned out to be kind of a hero after I had been kidnapped by a Bigfoot earlier in the summer. But Lucius had started picking on me long before that. In fact, it started the minute he met me.

My friend Brenda Connors suggested that maybe Lucius and I had been enemies in a past life. That sounded kind of silly to me, but who knows? I think he just hated my looks—I do wear glasses and have kind of a big nose. I also knew that I was sick of it.

So the last thing I needed when Lucius got me with the pudding was to have my crazy ghost friend Robert float down in front of me and say, "You know, Stuart, you really have to do something about that kid."

I just glared at him—partly because it was hardly what I'd call a news flash, and partly because by that time I'd learned that talking to Robert in public got me in trouble. This is mostly because no one but me can see him. The reason I can see him is that he lets me. But *why* he lets me is beyond me. Whenever I ask him, he just says something insulting, like that I'm the weirdest kid at camp and he figures I need all the friends I can get.

Even so, it's not easy to ignore Robert in situations like this. You can't just say, "We'll talk about it later," the way your parents do, because people will still think you're bonkers.

But I'm learning.

Fortunately we were all distracted about then because someone started shouting and screaming on the other side of the dining hall.

To my astonishment, it was Harry Housen. Harry was my favorite counselor at Camp Haunted Hills—a movie camp in southern Oregon. He was in charge of teaching my favorite subject—special effects. We had gotten to be friends when I found and returned his pet iguana, Myron, one night after the critter had wandered off.

Something was definitely wrong here. Harry was so mild mannered, I had once seen him apologize to a spider for having to move its web. I had seen him try to shoot the same scene dozens of times without losing his temper.

But from the way he was carrying on now you would have thought he hadn't just lost his temper but that someone had kidnapped it and was holding it for ransom.

"I can't take it anymore!" screamed Harry. "This place is driving me out of my mind!"

Suddenly he came bounding across the dining hall and jumped right onto my table. He grabbed a pitcher of bug juice—that's the stuff they give you to drink at camps—and poured in a little package of powder.

3

"You'll be sorry!" he cried, holding the pitcher straight out in front of him. "All of you will regret what you've done to me!"

I started to worry. Like me, Harry got picked on a lot. He was a tall, skinny guy with a big hooked nose. Flash Milligan, the camp's handsome lighting instructor was always making fun of him. Had Flash's teasing finally driven Harry over the deep end?

Now the pitcher was starting to bubble and steam. Within seconds, foam was pouring over the sides and onto the table.

"I'm going crazy I tell you!" screamed Harry. "CRAAAAAAZY!"

Everyone gasped as he raised the pitcher to his lips and took a deep drink of the stuff. The foaming brew poured down the front of his shirt. When he was done, he looked around wildly, then grabbed his throat and began to make weird, choking noises.

An instant later he fell to the floor and rolled under the table.

Chapter Two

Dr. Jekyll's Nephew

Harry had gotten hairy.

When he crawled out from under the table, just moments after he rolled under it, he had fur all over his hands and face. Not only that—he seemed to have grown fangs and claws, too.

He jumped to his feet and began snarling and snapping. The kids closest to him drew back, screaming.

"Everyone stay in your seats!" commanded Peter Flinches, the camp director. Peter was speaking over the bullhorn he sometimes used to call us to order. His voice boomed through the mess hall.

Suddenly Harry whirled around and ran for the door. I was dying to take off after him. After all, Harry was my friend. But Dan had put a hand on my shoulder to keep me in my seat. Sometimes I think that guy can read minds.

As Harry ran out of the mess hall he slammed

the door behind him, causing a big sign to roll down.

Harry Housen Presents
DR. JEKYLL'S NEPHEW

The Most Terrifying Film since
Abbott and Costello Meet Frankenstein

Filming starts Wednesday.
Casting begins tomorrow morning at ten.

Everyone began to laugh and cheer. This was one of the things that made Camp Haunted Hills so great; the staff was always pulling crazy stunts like this. Sometimes they did it just to scare us. Other times it was to make us think about something. Sometimes they were practicing their own moviemaking skills. And sometimes, as now, they did it to announce a new project.

I suppose a lot of the kids had figured out soon after it got started that Harry's tantrum was a joke. But I had learned early on that the best way to enjoy this kind of stuff was to let myself get swept up in it. I had been scared, and I had enjoyed it.

Unfortunately, not everyone at our table knew how to have a good time with this stuff.

Lucius was a good example. "What a geek," he said when things had finally quieted down. For

7

a moment I wasn't sure if he was talking about Harry or me, since Lucius called me a geek about fifteen times a day. Once I asked him if it was because it was the only good line he knew and he was afraid he'd forget it. He hit me, so I dropped the topic.

Anyway, I didn't think Harry was a geek. I thought he was about the most interesting person in the camp. And I had every intention of getting involved with his film.

After lunch we had some free time. Brenda and Eddie decided to walk with me while I went back to Bunk Thirteen to change my T-shirt.

I was glad Eddie was willing to be friends with Brenda. A lot of the guys don't like to hang around with girls. But Brenda was okay. For one thing, she was really brave. In fact, she had saved my life when the Sasquatch kidnapped me earlier in the summer. So I was willing to put up with some of the things about her that might have bugged me. At least she'd gotten rid of her braids.

We were about halfway to the bunk when we saw a big armored van come driving through the main gate.

"Wow. What do you suppose that is?" asked Eddie.

Eddie was very easily impressed.

"Probably a load of money," said Brenda.

That wouldn't have been as strange as it sounded. Camp Haunted Hills was created by Gregory Stevens, the most successful director in Hollywood. His new film, *Boogeymen*, had opened the week after camp started, and it was earning money so fast people had started joking that the government was going to have to open a new printing plant to make enough dollars to pay Gregory's earnings.

"I bet it's something for the Cottage," I said. "According to Harry, they're bringing in a lot of stuff for it this week."

The Cottage was what Gregory called the house he was building for himself on the hill that overlooked the lake. It was a cottage in about the same way King Kong was a gorilla; the shape was right, but the size wasn't what most people had in mind when they used the word.

In fact, this was probably going to be the most high-tech cottage in history. Camp was filled with rumors about the fabulous devices Gregory was supposed to be installing in the place—everything from wall-size televisions to electronic rugs. Don't ask me what an electronic rug is; I'm just telling you what people were saying.

"You guys are such dweebs," said a familiar voice behind us.

"Hey, Lucius learned a new word!" said Robert,

9

who was floating off to the right.

I tried to stifle my snort.

"What do you mean?" demanded Eddie, his freckles beginning to disappear as his face turned red.

Lucius laughed. "Because everyone in camp but you knows what's in that truck."

"Oh, yeah? Well, what is it?"

"It's *it*!" said Lucius significantly.

I caught my breath. Was it possible? In addition to the rumors about the high-tech stuff being brought in, people had been whispering about something else that Gregory had bought for the Cottage: a genuine Egyptian *mummy*.

"This I've got to see," said Robert, and he blinked out of sight.

I smiled. I knew I would get a full report later.

That's one of the good things about having a ghost for a friend; he can find out all kinds of interesting things you'd never be able to learn on your own.

But before you get too jealous, remember that coping with Robert had more than its share of problems, a fact of which I was soon to be reminded.

Chapter Three

The Script

Harry was painting Myron blue when I walked into the special-effects shop later that afternoon. He did this kind of thing occasionally, because he liked to use the iguana in the little movies he always made when he was experimenting with ideas for special effects.

. Myron, who was used to these indignities, was sprawled across the table with his eyes closed. I could see his sides moving slowly in and out as he breathed.

"Well, what did you think?" asked Harry, referring to his big scene in the dining hall.

"It was great!" I said. But I did feel a little hurt that Harry hadn't told me in advance what he was planning.

Harry must have read the expression on my face. "I thought about telling you what I was cooking up," he said. "But then I decided you might enjoy

11

it more if it was a surprise." He smiled, a big toothy grin. "You know how I like to surprise people."

It was true. Harry had told me once that his main goal in life was "to amaze, astound, and astonish as many people as possible."

"It's okay," I said, trying to sound casual, "as long as I get to work on the film."

"No question!" cried Harry. "I've been counting on you from the beginning to be my assistant."

I smiled. I never should have doubted Harry. He had learned weeks ago that he could count on me whenever he needed someone to help him with special effects. In fact, it was through working together that the two of us had gotten to be such good friends.

How good? Well, before the afternoon was over Harry had shown me about half the tricks he'd used to make the quick change under the table. That should tell you something. (I'd share them with you, but Harry swore me to secrecy.)

"But what's the new movie going to be about?" I asked, as he was pulling a fur-covered strip of latex off the back of his hand.

"Bad movies," he said with a smile.

"I don't get it."

"Bad movies. Rip-offs. All those lousy, I-don't-care-as-long-as-I-make-a-buck monster films that people have been churning out for the last fifty years." His face was serious. "Do you love monster movies, Stuart?"

"Of course I do," I said enthusiastically.

"Then the people who make *bad* monster movies, the people who don't care about what we love, should make you mad."

I began to understand what he was getting at. I had seen more than my share of lousy monster movies—more than anyone's share, according to my mother.

I nodded my head.

"Well, I want to make fun of them," said Harry, as if he were a general planning a major battle.

"Do you think that'll stop them?" I asked.

"Really, Stuart," said Robert, materializing above me, "you are incredibly simpleminded. Those people will never stop, as long as other people keep paying good money to see lousy movies."

I thought about asking Robert just when he had become an expert on economics, but I decided against it, since Harry still didn't know about my ghost friend.

"I know it won't stop them," said Harry. "But it'll make me feel better."

It took me a moment to realize he was answering my question. Trying to listen to Robert and carry on a conversation with someone else at the same time can really be confusing!

"I suppose next he's going to say, 'A man's got to do what a man's got to do,' " said Robert.

"Besides," said Harry, "a man's got to do what a man's got to do."

"That kind of thinking is what got me turned into a ghost," said Robert in disgust. He blinked out of sight.

That was frustrating! I often wondered how Robert had died. But the one time I actually asked him, he accused me of being rude and refused to tell me, which made me even more curious.

"Do you want to see the script?" asked Harry, distracting me from my cranky thoughts about Robert.

"Sure!"

"Wait here," he said, disappearing into his secret room, the one at the back of the special-effects lab with the words KEEP OUT! TOP SECRET! painted on the door in big red letters.

As far as I knew, I was the only camper who had been allowed in that room. It was one of my favorite places on earth, a wonderland of gadgets and glop for making every kind of special effect imaginable.

"You'll have to read it here," said Harry, returning with the script. "I'm keeping it a secret for now."

I didn't see what the point was of keeping a script

14

secret if we were going to start filming it in just a couple of days. Finally I decided Harry was just imitating his hero, Gregory Stevens, who was a fanatic about keeping his films secret until their premieres.

Which reminded me—

"Are you ready for Friday night?" I asked.

Harry actually turned white. "I'm ready," he said. "But I'm not looking forward to it. I belong *behind* the camera. I don't like to talk in front of audiences."

I nodded in sympathy. When Gregory Stevens had announced that he wanted to celebrate the opening of the new Camp Haunted Hills theater with a special preview of *Cry of the Sasquatch*, it sounded really exciting. When he announced that the film would be followed by a panel discussion, it sounded a little less exciting. When he announced that the panel would consist of the people who had made the film—including me as the young Sasquatch and Harry as the director—it got downright scary.

But I had gotten used to the idea; obviously Harry hadn't.

I forgot about Harry's worries as I started reading his script. Before long I was chuckling to myself. By the time I was done, I was slapping the table and howling. His script was really funny, and it was *filled* with great special effects. I couldn't wait to start working on it.

"Not bad," said Robert.

His voice startled me. I looked around and realized that he'd been reading over my shoulder.

"We can have some fun with this," he continued. "I can't wait to get to work."

I shuddered. Anytime Robert gets that excited about something, trouble is sure to follow.

Chapter Four

What Robert Saw

Later that evening Brenda and I were walking from the social hall back toward the bunk houses.

"What the heck is this?" asked Brenda, as we walked past the trail leading up to Gregory Steven's cottage.

She bent to pick up something she had spotted beside the path. She turned it over in her hand, examining it carefully. I tried to see what she had found, but the sun was just setting, and it was too dark to make out more than the general shape of the thing.

"Well, what is it?" I asked at last.

"I don't know," she said. She handed it to me. "It looks like some kind of bug."

Whatever it was, the thing was heavy. I held it up, trying to catch the last rays of the sun. Brenda was right: it was shaped like a bug—like a beetle,

to be more precise. It seemed to be made of some kind of yellowish metal. It gleamed dully in the last bit of light.

"I bet it's something the kids in the prop classes made," I said. I flipped it over and rubbed my thumb across the huge stone set between the beetle's wings. "I can ask Keith Carter to check it out for us."

Keith was a kid we had met in Harry's special-effects class the first week of camp.

"I doubt they care," said Brenda. "They're always leaving junk around. I think they do it to bug people. Sheila found a fake eyeball lying on the beach last week and nearly went out of her mind."

"Sheila's nearly out of her mind, anyway," I said.

Brenda frowned. "I like Sheila," she said. "Anyway, this gold bug is a lot better than an eyeball. You ask Keith about it. But in the meantime I'm going to hold on to it."

I shrugged. That was fine with me. We came to the place where our paths separated. I looked around and was relieved to see that no one was watching us. I like Brenda. But if I got too friendly with her, people would start teasing me.

Sometimes I get so sick of that stuff I could puke. What happened next is a good example. No sooner had I walked away from Brenda than you-know-who popped up in front of me.

"Well," said Robert, "now that your girlfriend's gone, we can talk."

See what I mean?

"Brenda's not my girlfriend!" I said.

"Listen to him," said Robert, rolling his eyes heavenward. "And he used to be such an honest boy!"

I kept walking, which meant that I walked right through the spot where Robert was standing. I felt a little chill of cold as I passed through him, but nothing more.

"Oh, cute," said Robert, turning to float after me. "That's very clever of you, Stuart. I guess you don't want to hear about Gregory Stevens's mummy after all."

I stopped. "Oh, I suppose I might," I said, trying not to sound too eager. If Robert knew how excited I really was, he would drag this out forever, just to annoy me.

"Well, if you're not interested—" he said with a shrug.

Obviously he was going to tease me, anyway.

"I'm interested! I'm interested!" I yelled. Then I quickly looked around to see if anyone had heard me shouting to myself. "So talk," I hissed between my teeth.

Robert chuckled mercilessly. But he was too

filled with his news to keep me in suspense for long.

"Well," he said, "I went floating into the Cottage after that truck passed us this afternoon. Your buddy Lucius was right—"

"Don't call him my buddy," I said.

Robert just grinned.

"Will you get on with your story?" I said at last.

"Well, to begin with, you ought to see the inside of that place. It has three times as much room underground as it does above. There's an indoor pool down there, with a waterfall running into it, and a private theater. I saw—"

"Does it have electronic rugs?" I asked.

Robert looked at me as if I were from another planet. "I don't have the slightest idea," he said. "But it does have theme rooms. One room is decorated like something out of an old cowboy movie. Another one looks as if it was used by pirates. There's a space room and one about ancient Egypt. That's where they put the mummy, of course."

"Of course," I said.

"Anyway, here's the exciting part. After these two guys walked in with the mummy case, one of them opened it and took something out of it."

"You mean he stole something!" I gasped.

Robert nodded solemnly.

21

"That's disgusting," I said.

"I agree," said Robert. "We dead people have rights, too."

Actually, I had been thinking that whatever the deliveryman had taken had really been stolen from Mr. Stevens. But I decided not to say that to Robert.

"Why didn't you stop him?" I asked.

Robert gave me that look again. "Now how was I supposed to do that?" he said.

"Couldn't you have scared him?"

"I'm not that kind of ghost," said Robert. He sounded offended. "I don't make a habit of appearing to strangers, you know."

I pointed out that I was a stranger the first time he appeared to me.

"That was different," said Robert. "I only did that so we could be friends."

I gave up. By this time I knew Robert well enough to know that I could argue with him like this all night without getting anywhere. But I couldn't figure out what to do about it. If I tried to report that something had been stolen, they'd ask how I knew. If I told them I had learned it from a ghost—well, you can imagine how they'd react.

I was still trying to figure out what to do when we got back to Bunk Thirteen.

"Well, I'll see you tomorrow." said Robert. He

was unusually cheerful, which should have made me suspicious right away.

"See you tomorrow," I said softly, in case anyone might be listening.

Robert was just fading out of sight when Eddie Mayhew stuck his head out the door. "Hey, Stuart!" he yelled. "Stop talking to yourself and get in here. Lucius is painting your underwear."

Chapter Five

Robert Helps Out

I had eight pairs of underwear—one for each day of the week and one extra to wear while the others were being washed.

The seven pairs I wasn't wearing were laid across my bunk. One word had been written on each pair, so that when they were all put together they said, "Please return to Stuart Glassman, Bunk 13," in bright red letters. Lucius stood in front of the underwear with a paintbrush in his hand, admiring his work.

"Hi, Glassman," he said when I walked in. "I know you have a hard time keeping track of things. So I thought I'd give you a hand."

I thought maybe I should give Lucius a hand by punching him in the head. But he's a lot bigger than I am. So I just sighed and started to pick up my underwear.

"Aren't you going to thank me?" asked Lucius.

I could feel myself blushing. The other kids were laughing. I was so mad my eyes were stinging. It was all I could do to keep from crying. But I didn't want to get in a fight with him right then. I really hate fights—mostly because I always lose.

So I just picked up the underwear and stuffed it back into my trunk, making a vow to myself that I would never, never, never leave the trunk unlocked again.

Actually, the bit with the underwear was really just one more skirmish in the ongoing battle between Lucius and me. Normally I try not to get involved in that kind of thing. But you can get dumped on only so many times before you have to stand up for yourself. So along with a couple of my friends (mainly Eddie Mayhew and Brenda Connors) I had been trying to take a stand against the creep.

The problem was, no matter what we did, Lucius would come up with something worse. He didn't seem to think it was possible to just call things a draw at some point. It may sound as if we weren't willing to stop, either. But we had tried to. Lucius just kept tormenting us, anyway.

According to my father, it's situations like this that make world peace impossible. My feeling is that if people like Lucius are running the world, I'd like to find another planet to call home.

After I finished putting away my underwear, I expected Robert to pop up and tell me that I had to do something about all this.

Little did I know that he had already decided to take matters into his own hands!

The trouble started three days later—Wednesday, the first day of filming for *Dr. Jekyll's Nephew.* To my total disgust, Lucius had been cast in the title role. I suppose if you believe in typecasting, it made a certain amount of sense. And to be honest, he did *look* right for the role—even the human part.

But I was eager to see what our beautiful makeup specialist, Aurora Jackson, had in mind for the monster part. I knew that whatever monsterish look she came up with would be more suited to the *personality* of the Lucius I knew and despised.

Unfortunately, I was late for the first day of filming because Splash Calhoun, our waterfront director, kept me late for a little extra instruction.

I was going to represent the camp in a big swim meet we had coming up. Splash wanted me to swim well, and I wanted to swim well, too. But, mainly, I was dying to get over to Harry's studio.

When Splash finally let me go, I dried off, threw

on my clothes, and almost split a side running up to Harry's studio.

Robert greeted me at the door.

"You can relax, Stuart," he said. "Everything's taken care of."

"What do you mean?" I asked.

But he just chuckled and wouldn't say anything else. I should have known then we were in for trouble. But in my wildest dreams I wouldn't have guessed how much.

Everything went pretty smoothly for the first couple of hours. Being late didn't make that much difference, really; if you ever get involved in making a film, the first thing you'll learn is that setting up takes forever. At least it seems that way. It all has to do with getting the lights and the camera angles just right—important stuff, I suppose, since otherwise you wouldn't be able to see anything when the film is shown. But it can be dull to sit through.

The kids doing the acting in the film were sitting around chatting with one another. Well, most of them were chatting. Lucius was bragging about how great he was going to be. Aurora was sitting at a table off to the side, putting finishing touches on her sketches for the makeup. Flash Milligan, who was sort of a grown-up version of Lucius, was

27

putting up the lights and telling Harry what a favor he was doing by helping out on the film.

"This is incredibly boring," said Robert. "Wake me up when we get to the good part."

"What do you mean, 'the good part'?" I asked nervously.

But Robert just smiled and faded out of sight, leaving me to wonder what he had in mind.

Chapter Six

Lucius Colton, Star

As it turned out, we didn't get to "the good part" until after supper. We had one technical delay after another. The situation wasn't helped any by the fact that Flash and Harry were both trying to show off for Aurora, which meant that they kept getting into arguments about the best way to do anything.

I was actually beginning to nod off when Harry pulled me over and said, "Stuart, will you run the mist machine?"

"Sure!" I said. I loved the mist machine. Harry had taught me how to use it one night when we were working on one of his secret projects. The next day my arms ached from the way I had pumped the handle to make clouds of mysterious-looking mist pour into the room. But it had made me feel neat—as if I were in charge of the weather or something.

I was setting up the machine when Brenda sidled over to talk to me.

"Has Lucius been sneaking out of the bunk at night?" she asked me.

"Not that I know of," I said. When I finished pouring the mist fluid into the machine I stood up and asked her why she wanted to know.

Brenda shrugged. "We heard weird noises outside our bunk last night," she said. "I figured it was probably Lucius trying to scare us."

"I wouldn't put it past him," I said, "but as far as I can remember he was in the bunk, being obnoxious all night long."

She shrugged. "Did you ask Keith about that bug-thing I found?" she asked.

I slapped my head. "I forgot," I said, feeling embarrassed. "I'll ask him tomorrow."

"Brenda, I need you," said Aurora.

"This should be fun," she whispered. "We're about to turn Lucius into a monster."

I took my place beside the mist machine and settled in to watch.

Harry blew his whistle, which was the only way to get everyone's attention at once.

"We're going to make a test shot," he announced, "so we can get an idea of how the transformation will work onscreen. If you're involved

in the technical end take your place. If you're acting, just stay out of the way for now. Lucius, get
in position."

Smirking as if he were the king of the world,
Lucius ambled over to the spot Harry had indi-
cated.

"Good!" said Robert, popping up beside me,
"this is the part I've been waiting for."

"What do you mean?" I whispered.

But Robert just put his finger to his lips. "Shhh!"
he hissed. "Do you want people to think you're
crazy?"

How annoying can you get? His favorite game
was to try to get me to talk to him when other
people were around.

"Now you all know the story of Dr. Jekyll and
Mr. Hyde," said Harry.

That was certainly true; Harry had arranged for
us to see four different film versions of it over the
past two nights. Some people got bored. Not me;
I can sit and watch that kind of thing all night
long. I never got tired of watching that kindly Eng-
lish doctor drink the mysterious potion that un-
leashed his evil side. I had been having fantasies
about inventing a potion like that, myself; I figured
it might help me deal with Lucius.

Harry was still talking. "This story is about Dr.

Jekyll's nephew—a mild-mannered kid who discovers his uncle's secret formula and gets in all kinds of trouble as a result. In the scene we're going to try now, he's out on a London street. Fog has moved in and is swirling around him. He decides to try the potion for the first time. We'll film up to that point, and then we'll shut off the camera so that Aurora can start the makeup job."

He smiled at Aurora. I groaned at the sappy grin on his face. Obviously he still had a crush on her— like most of the adult males in camp.

Actually, most of the campers had crushes on her, too.

"Now, here's your potion, Lucius," said Harry as he poured a batch of his frothing Dr. Jekyll powder into a beaker of water. He had explained to me earlier that it was nothing but a couple of harmless chemicals that created all the froth and foam. Even so, the effect was pretty spectacular.

"Okay, Stuart," yelled Harry. "Give me some mist!"

I started pumping for all I was worth. After about thirty seconds the pressure built up and the machine began to hiss. Suddenly a thick white mist began to seep out of the nozzle. It crept across the floor and began to curl around Lucius's feet.

"More mist!" cried Harry.

I started pumping harder. I felt as if my arm was going to come off. Working that machine was tough!

"Perfect, Stuart," yelled Harry. "Now, Lucius—take the beaker and drink the potion in one big gulp."

"You're going to like what happens next," said Robert, as my enemy downed the bubbling brew. "It should be really funny."

I looked at Robert in horror. Lucius may be my enemy, but Robert in a playful mood is something I wouldn't wish on anyone.

I looked around. Everyone else was watching Lucius, so it was safe to talk.

"What do you mean?" I whispered nervously.

"Just watch," said Robert smugly. "You'll see."

So I watched. And I saw.

First Lucius downed the potion.

Then Harry yelled, "Okay, shut off the camera. Lucius hold your position. Aurora, give him the first coat of makeup."

But before Aurora could take a step, *the transformation started all by itself.*

It was amazing. One minute Lucius was just a normal kid—at least, as normal as he'll ever get. The next minute he had dark circles around his eyes and was sprouting hair on the tips of his ears.

"Isn't that neat!" said Robert cheerfully. "I told you this was going to be good."

Good was the wrong word. *Terrifying* would have been more like it.

Chapter Seven

The Transformation
of Lucius Colton

For a moment no one said a thing. We were all too stunned by what was happening.

Then several things happened nearly at once.

First Aurora got mad. "Look," she said, stomping over to a baffled-looking Harry, "if you wanted to do the makeup on your own, all you had to do was say so. You didn't need to set up some trick to prove what a great special-effects artist you are. I know you're good. But I'm good, too. Why didn't you just tell me you were going to handle this on your own?"

Harry looked as if he had just been hit between the eyes with a baseball bat. I felt sorry for him. On one side of him he had his star turning into a monster all by himself, and on the other side he had the woman he was in love with, blaming him for doing it.

"But, Aurora—" said Harry.

He was interrupted by a growl from Lucius. Everyone's attention turned back to him. I could almost hear what they were thinking: *Oh, that was clever. Harry and Aurora had a fight to take our attention away from Lucius while he put on a little more makeup.*

We were getting wise to the Camp Haunted Hills style. After four weeks everyone had started to figure out how things worked. Considering some of the stunts the staff had pulled already, it was a lot easier to believe that you were seeing a trick than it was to believe that the kid in front of you was turning into a monster.

Unless you counted Robert and Lucius, I was the only one in the room who knew what was happening. Or to put it another way, I was the only normal person in the room who knew that Lucius really *was* turning into a monster.

And I do mean a monster. By now his face was almost entirely covered with fur. His ears were pointier than Mr. Spock's. His twitching lips revealed a pair of fangs that would have looked good on Ralph the Wonder Wolf. His shirt was tight, and I realized it was because of the bulging muscles forming underneath it.

"Nice job, Harry," said Aurora bitterly. She

37

stalked past me. Mist swirled around her feet as she crossed the studio. She slammed the door on the way out.

"Tsk, tsk," said Robert from somewhere over my head. "It's amazing how professional jealousy can blind a person to reality."

Personally, I was feeling sorry for Harry, since this certainly wasn't going to do him any good in his pursuit of the beautiful Aurora. But I didn't have much time to worry about my friend's love life, because about two seconds later Lucius went berserk.

"Eerrnnaarggghhh!" he growled, and started running toward Mike Burrows. Mike shouted and ran away from him.

"Hey, Lucius," someone else cried, "over here!"

The others still didn't realize what was going on! They thought this was part of the setup, a game of tag with the monster.

I watched in horror as Lucius went careening through the mist that still filled the studio. He was leaping from table to table, bounding over chairs, growling and snapping at the kids—who were screaming and shouting and giggling in delight as they ran from him. What saved them was that there were so many of them, and Lucius didn't seem able to concentrate on any one kid. Just as he was about to grab someone, another kid would

38

call his name and he'd go leaping off after him or her instead.

From the sound of his howls and growls, I suspected he was finding the "game" increasingly frustrating. I shuddered to think what might happen if he actually got his hands on one of the kids.

"Robert!" I hissed. "This is your fault. Do something!"

"Why don't you do something first?" he replied. "Something useful, like turning on the camera."

Well, by this time I had heard plenty of talk about not wasting a good film opportunity. Besides, I knew I wouldn't get any more information out of that ghost until I had done what he suggested. So I waded through the mist and flipped the switch that started the camera.

"Of course, if Harry had any brains," said Robert, who was floating along behind me, "he would just give Lucius the antidote."

"What antidote?" I cried.

Robert pointed over to a table in the middle of the set, where I could see a second beaker filled with bright green liquid. It was clearly labeled ANTIDOTE.

I grabbed the bottle and started toward Harry to tell him what to do. But before I had taken two steps, some fool opened the door and Lucius went barreling out of the building.

"Hey, wait!" I yelled. "I have the antidote!"

But it was too late. Lucius was gone.

Now here was a situation: my best friend (that was Robert's term for himself, not mine) had just turned my worst enemy into a monster; that monster had just escaped from the studio; I was holding the antidote to his condition in my hands; even worse, I was the only one in the room—aside from Robert—who understood that what was going on was *real*, and not some kind of joke.

As far as I could see, there was only one thing to do. As much as I disliked Lucius, I couldn't leave him like that.

So I went running after him.

Chapter Eight

The Forest at Night

I wonder if monsters have some kind of natural attraction for dark places. I mean, Lucius could have headed for the center of camp, where the light from the buildings would have made it easy to spot him. He could have headed for the waterfront, where the moonlight reflecting off the lake would have made him easy to see.

But did he run to any of these places?

No-o-o-o!

He headed straight for the forest.

When I reached the edge of the woods, I hesitated. I could hear Lucius crashing through the brush just ahead of me, but the forest was dark and spooky looking. And at the moment, Lucius *was* a monster. Who knew what he might do if I caught up with him?

On the other hand, since Robert had caused the whole mess, I felt as if I was at least partially responsible. Don't ask me why. Robert is at least ten years older than I am—older than that, if you count the time he's been dead. But I think his personality got frozen in place when he cashed in his chips. It always seemed that he was the kid and I was the grown-up. After just a few weeks of being his friend, I was beginning to understand how parents must feel.

I closed my eyes, took a deep breath, and plunged into the forest.

It was as dark and spooky as I had expected. I could hear Lucius howling somewhere ahead of me. Tightening my grip on the bottle of antidote, I headed in his direction.

After a moment I realized the bottle was actually glowing. That was a relief. I had rushed off without a flashlight or anything. But the glowing antidote shed enough light so that I could see a few feet around me, even in the darkest part of the forest.

Fog curled around my feet. It looked as if someone had been operating a giant mist machine in the woods. The dew-covered leaves left trails of dampness as they brushed across my cheeks. The night air was heavy with that special forest smell of decaying matter and damp earth. It was even stronger now than it was in the daytime.

There's something strange and magical about a forest at night. Go into one and tell me that you don't hear a monster lurking behind every tree. Things can get very scary, very fast.

Especially when you suddenly hear a branch snap *behind* you.

I looked over my shoulder, but I couldn't see anyone.

Great. A dark forest. A monster ahead of me. Something else—who knew what—behind me. A glowing beaker in my hand. The probability that a ghost would be showing up before long, too. Life couldn't get much more interesting.

At the moment I would gladly have settled for boredom.

"Lucius!" I yelled. "Lucius, come back! I have the antidote!"

I heard more crashing in the brush ahead, but it was still moving away from me. I wondered if Lucius was running away because he was embarrassed, because he didn't trust me about the antidote, or because he was planning to circle around so he could jump me from behind.

I jumped, myself, when I heard another branch snap behind me. I spun around and cried out in surprise as I saw who had been following me.

It was Brenda. She was out of breath, and her face appeared slightly green in the glow from the antidote.

"You scared me!" I hissed.

"Well, I'll go back if you want," she said angrily. "Everyone but Harry thinks this is just another joke, and *he's* so confused he doesn't know what to think. I'm the only one who figured out you actually meant it when you ran off raving about having the antidote. If you want me to go back, I'll be glad to. Running around the woods at night is not my idea of a good time."

I shook my head. "I'm glad you're here," I said. And I meant it. "You scared me, that's all."

We heard a howl somewhere ahead of us.

"Speaking of being scared—" said Brenda nervously.

"I know," I said. "But we can't leave him like this. Come on. Let's see if we can find him."

"What are we going to do if we do find him?" she asked. "How can we get him to drink the antidote?"

"I don't know," I said grimly. "We'll just have to try and see what happens."

She nodded. I pushed aside a branch and started forward again.

We traveled in silence for a little while. It started to rain, nothing more than a soft sprinkle that pattered lightly on the leaves. The moon moved in and out of the clouds, and Brenda and I moved in and out of patches of moonlight and darkness. After a while she spoke again.

"Stuart," she said.

"Yeah?"

"What's going on around here? I know this isn't just another Camp Haunted Hills stunt, any more than that Bigfoot who kidnapped you was. I've been watching you. You act really strange sometimes—as if you can see something no one else sees. It scares me a little. Everyone else just thinks you're weird—I suppose maybe you are—but I also know it's something more. What is it? What do you see that I can't?"

I hesitated. Could I tell Brenda about Robert? What would she say if I did? What would *he* say if I did? He had made it pretty clear that he didn't want anyone else to know about him. But if that was so, then he shouldn't keep pulling stupid stunts like this.

I was just deciding that I didn't give a hoot what Robert thought when I heard Lucius howling somewhere off to the right.

"Come on," I said, taking Brenda's hand. "Let's see if we can catch a monster."

I lifted the glowing beaker like a lantern, and we moved through the darkened forest toward the sound of Lucius's howling.

Chapter Nine

Monster Hunt

The problem is, I thought half an hour later, *Lucius can travel faster than we can.* I wasn't certain, but I had a feeling he was actually swinging through the trees. From what I had seen back in the studio, there was no question that he had muscles that would put mine to shame. A Tarzan act should be no problem for Lucius now.

In fact, I began to suspect that the only reason we were keeping up with him was that every once in a while he'd stop and wait for us. I wondered if the human side of Lucius was having a battle with the monster side and trying to convince it that help was on the way.

I certainly hoped the human side would win out. But remembering Lucius, I thought the odds were against it. So I was getting pretty worried about what was going to happen when we ran into him. Generally speaking, I wouldn't want to run into

Lucius on a dark night even when he's in a good mood.

"Lucius!" I yelled. "Lucius, it's me, Stuart. I have an antidote. I can change you back!"

No answer. The only sound was the rain pattering on the leaves.

"Do you suppose something happened to him?" asked Brenda nervously.

"I doubt it," I said. "In the shape he's in now, if he met a bear and got into a fight, the bear would be in big trouble."

"But maybe he fell over a cliff or something," said Brenda.

I paused. That seemed possible. Lucius certainly wasn't thinking clearly. In his mad rampage through the forest it seemed only too possible that he might not pay much attention to where he was going.

Fortunately—or unfortunately—I didn't have to worry about it for long. All of a sudden we heard a terrible growling and snarling behind us. A second later, Lucius came bursting through the trees, slobbering and snorting and reaching out his hairy hands to grab us.

"*Run!*" yelled Brenda.

It was the most obvious advice I had ever gotten. Clutching the green beaker, I headed through the trees—with Lucius hot on my tail.

47

What do I do now? I thought desperately. *If I stop and try to give him the antidote, he'll probably do something terrible to me before I have a chance to get it down his throat.*

That, of course, was assuming that I could figure out *how* to get it down his throat if I did let him catch up with me.

Suddenly I stumbled. I dropped the beaker. Fortunately it landed on a soft pile of leaves and didn't break. I was thankful for the cork that kept the antidote from spilling. But as I was bending down to pick up the beaker, Lucius caught up with me.

For a moment I thought my life was over. He was snarling and slobbering. One side of his shirt had been ripped open, revealing a hairy arm, thick with muscles. His fingers were tipped with long, sharp claws that looked as if they could rip open my skin with no trouble at all.

I started to scream. But just as Lucius was about to grab me, a stone came crashing through the leaves and hit his back. He whirled around and took off in the direction he'd come from. I was so shaken up, it took me a moment to realize that it was Brenda who had smacked him with the rock. Now he was after her.

It's amazing what we'll do for a friend. Brenda had saved me, and I couldn't leave her to Lucius. So I started off after them. Luckily, I had gone only

48

a few feet when I heard a small voice whisper, "Stuart, over here!"

It was Brenda. She was hiding behind a clump of bushes. I ducked in next to her.

"He ran right past me," she whispered. "Whatever else that potion did, it didn't improve his sense of smell. I was afraid he'd track me down just with his nose."

"You don't smell *that* bad," I said, trying to make a joke.

She punched me in the arm. "Don't be such a smart aleck," she hissed. "What are we going to *do*?"

"I don't know," I said. "This antidote won't do any good if we can't get Lucius to drink it."

"Where did you get it, anyway?" she asked.

I swallowed. Here it was again—the big question: Should I tell her about Robert, or not?

Before I could answer, Brenda wrinkled her nose—I could see it in the dim, green glow from the beaker—and said, "What's that? It smells awful!"

I sniffed the air and almost gagged. As I said before, I love the earthy odor of the forest at night. But the pleasant smell had been replaced by that of a stronger kind of decay.

If death has a smell, I thought, *this must be it.*

I turned toward the stench, then shouted in fear at what I saw.

Shambling toward us through the brush was a large, human shape, wrapped head-to-toe in bandages.

Brenda grabbed my arm.

"It's the mummy!" she whispered, her voice husky with fear. "The mummy that Mr. Stevens bought. But what's it doing out here?"

"I don't know," I said. "And I don't want to find out. Let's just get out of here!"

"Unnnhhh!" groaned the mummy, lurching closer toward us.

We broke away from the bush and started to run. I stopped. A horrible howling had broken out behind us. It was Lucius. I turned and saw him charge straight at the mummy.

Great, I thought. *All we need is Robert to make things complete.*

"Well, this is interesting," said a familiar voice behind me.

I groaned. Now we had it all: a dark, misty night, thick woods, a monster, a mummy, *and* a ghost. I didn't see how things could get any worse.

That was when the first bolt of lightning sizzled across the sky. Two seconds later the crash of thunder almost knocked me off my feet. The skies opened and suddenly rain started to fall so hard it felt like a lake being dumped onto my head.

Sometimes life is so interesting I can't stand it.

Chapter Ten

Brenda Meets Robert

The sudden downpour had an unexpected side-effect: the mummy screamed and began heading away from us.

"Wimp," said Robert scornfully. "Can't you take a little water?"

I looked at him. "If you were as old as that mummy, you'd probably worry about getting wet, too."

Why I stopped to argue with him about a thing like that I don't know, except that by now I was so angry with him I guess I wasn't willing to let anything pass.

"Stuart, *who* are you talking to?" Brenda asked.

Great. I had done it again. But things were moving too fast for me to try wriggling out of it now. Once the mummy had taken off, Lucius turned his attention back to us.

Another bolt of lightning streaked through the night, illuminating the scene in a bright, white glare. Thunder shook the earth as Lucius crouched and began stalking toward us like some great animal that has cornered its prey.

"Put the potion down in front of you and back up slowly," said Robert.

"What good will that do?" I asked. I decided I didn't care what Brenda heard. Either she'd think I was nuts, which would be my problem, or she'd believe me when I told her I had been talking to a ghost, which would be Robert's problem. Whatever happened, I had too many other things to worry about right now.

"Lucius should be very thirsty," said Robert. "I expect he'll pick it up and drink it."

I placed the flask on a flat stone and pulled out the cork. Then I began slowly backing away.

Lucius continued to stalk me, growling softly as he came.

"Stuart, let's get out of here," Brenda said urgently.

"Don't run!" said Robert. "Just go slowly. He'll be more interested in the potion than in you, if you don't attract his attention."

"What makes you so sure he's thirsty?" I asked.

"I laced the Jekyll juice with salt," said Robert

proudly. "It was the only thing I could think to do to be sure he'd want to take the antidote."

"Wasn't that clever of you?" I said.

"I thought so," said Robert, sounding cheerful.

"*Who* are you talking to?" hissed Brenda as we took another soggy step backward.

"Shhh," I said.

Lucius had reached the antidote. He paused, then snatched up the bottle and poured the green liquid down his throat, gulping it greedily. Suddenly he began to cough and sputter. Grabbing at his throat, he flung himself to the ground and started to roll around.

I saw this happen only because of another streak of lightning. Once the glowing potion had disappeared down Lucius's throat, the forest was almost completely dark. Instantly a new terror took hold of me. What if the potion didn't work? Lucius might still be a monster, for all I knew. I screamed as I felt a touch on my arm. It was only Brenda.

Suddenly one more streak of lightning zigzagged across the night sky. By its light I saw Lucius—a very human Lucius—lying quietly on the forest floor, his skin pale, his hair plastered down by the rain.

I rushed forward but stumbled over a root in the darkness.

"Robert, give me some light, dammit!"

"Don't be so touchy," said Robert, shimmering into sight. As always happened when I saw him at night, he cast a soft glow around him.

"Stuart," said Brenda, "who are you—"

She stopped in midsentence. I heard her swallow. "Stuart," she said softly, "is that what I think it is?" She ran a hand across her eyes to wipe away the water.

The fear in her voice was so powerful, it made me remember the first time I had met Robert myself, and I shivered sympathetically.

"Yes, it is," I said. "His name is Robert, and he's sort of a friend of mine."

"Sort of!" said Robert. "Well, I like that. Save a guy's life and I'm 'sort of' a friend. That's gratitude for you."

I was only half listening to his cranky babble. First I wanted to make sure that Lucius was still breathing. It was hard to tell with the rain pounding down around us, but when I put my hand above his mouth I could feel air moving in and out.

What a relief. Little as I liked Lucius, I didn't want him dead!

"Come on," I said to Brenda. "Let's see if we can get him on his feet."

No answer.

"Brenda, give me a hand with Lucius, will you?"

No answer. I looked up. In the dim light of Rob-

ert's glow, I could see Brenda staring at my ghostly friend with fixed, terrified eyes.

"Buh—buh—buh," she said, her mouth flapping open and closed.

"Great," I said to Robert. "Now see what you've done? Why did you suddenly decide to let her see you?"

He shrugged. "You were the one who kept blabbing in front of her."

"Well, how was I *supposed* to talk to you?" I snapped.

"Who said you had to talk?" replied Robert. "You could have just shut up and done what I told you."

This conversation was getting entirely too cranky for my taste. I stood up and put my arm around Brenda's shoulder. "It's all right," I said. "He's a friendly ghost. Sort of like Casper."

"Oh, puh-leeeze!" groaned Robert. "If I were alive, I'd puke."

"But—buh—buh," said Brenda, finally raising a hand to point at Robert. She was making progress.

"Brenda," I said, shaking her. "Brenda, it's okay!"

Of course, that was stretching things a little. Things were far from okay. And I couldn't really blame her. The only reason I hadn't been this scared the first time I met Robert was that I had thought he was a joke, some kind of three-dimen-sional picture that the staff had cooked up. Poor Brenda had already dealt with a monster and a mummy that night. Asking her to cope with a ghost, too, really didn't seem fair.

Suddenly I heard a voice call my name.

"Oh, oh," said Robert. "Company!"

He blinked out of sight, leaving me in the dark, in the pouring rain, with Lucius unconscious in front of me and Brenda nearly out of her mind with fear beside me.

Chapter Eleven

The Morning After

"Stuart," said Harry, stepping out from between two trees. "I've been looking all over for you! Are you all right?"

He was carrying a large halogen flashlight. I hadn't been that glad to see anyone since—well, since Brenda drove the camp van into the clearing where the Sasquatch were holding me prisoner.

But Harry's arrival wasn't without complications. Such as, did I want to tell him about what was going on, or not? My mind was racing so fast that if it had been a car, it might have lifted off the road and taken to the air. If I told Harry what was really going on, would he believe me? Probably not. If he didn't, what would happen? Well, maybe he would get mad at me for "lying" (even though I was telling the truth). Or maybe he would decide that I was cracking up. And if he did believe me—

what then? I couldn't begin to imagine his reaction, which made me suspect it was unlikely that Harry would believe me.

Trying to figure all this out kept my mouth shut just long enough for me to learn something really valuable: people are so eager to have the world make sense that they are more willing to rearrange what their senses have told them than they are to rearrange their thinking.

"Of course!" said Robert when I mentioned this idea to him the next day. "That's one of my favorite things about people. It lets me get away with all kinds of stuff."

I got a perfect demonstration of this when Harry pointed his flashlight at me and said, "Listen, Stuart, I know you were mad at me for not letting you in on my Dr. Jekyll bit in the dining hall the other day. But I don't think it was fair for you to disrupt the whole shooting schedule like this just to get back at me."

My jaw dropped. Harry actually thought Lucius and I had planned this whole disaster! I didn't know which was more laughable: the idea that I really could have done something like this, or the idea that Lucius and I could have cooperated long enough to pull it off.

"I must admit," continued Harry, "that once I settled down a little, I was proud of you—and even

60

a little jealous. You've taken some of my tricks and added your own touches."

Just then Lucius groaned.

Harry pointed his flashlight in the direction of the sound. "What happened to him?" he cried.

"He fell and hit his head," I said, which I figured was probably true, if only barely. "That's part of why we were out here so long."

Harry nodded. "I figured something had gone wrong when you didn't come right back. He knelt beside Lucius. Using his thumb, he pulled up one of Lucius's eyelids and pointed the flashlight into his face.

"Hey!" yelled Lucius. "Cut that out."

Well, from the sound of things, he was going to be okay. But as we led Lucius out of the woods, I could tell the last hour was pretty foggy for him. He knew he had been doing something strange, but he wasn't quite sure what it was.

Harry seemed to think his fogginess was part of our act, which was just fine as far as I was concerned.

Robert had disappeared when Harry arrived. As soon as he was gone, Brenda seemed to recover from the worst of her fear. She stuck pretty close to me as we made our way out of the woods. But at least she could walk and talk.

Unfortunately, the first words out of her mouth

were "You have a lot of explaining to do, Stuart Glassman." This was whispered to me as we were walking side by side behind Harry and Lucius on a narrow part of the trail.

What's to explain? I thought. *My best friend is a ghost. As soon as I tell you that, you'll know as much as I do.*

However, something told me Brenda wasn't going to settle for that explanation. She was going to want *details.*

She made this clear the next morning at breakfast. The previous night we had been too wet and tired for the conversation we both knew was coming. But just as I was trying to dip my toast into my fried egg—an obvious waste of time, since I hadn't found a soft yolk since I'd arrived at Camp Haunted Hills—Brenda leaned back from her table and dug her elbow into my ribs to tell me that she wanted to have a major conversation with me after breakfast.

I sighed. I did have one consolation, though. Lucius was relatively subdued that morning. And it was really funny to watch the baffled expression on his face when kids came up to congratulate him on his great performance. However, being Lucius, he quickly rose to the occasion; he even had the nerve to brag about it!

As my grandmother says, some people have no shame.

While most of the kids were impressed with Lucius, Aurora Jackson was definitely cool to him. It took me a little while to figure out that this was because she still thought the whole episode was something Harry had cooked up to show off, and that Lucius had been in cahoots with him.

I glanced over at Harry. He was aimlessly pushing his food around his plate, and staring at it as though he were watching some terrible tragedy.

It's sights like this that have convinced me I should never fall in love.

"Talk," said Brenda, as everyone stood up to leave. "Now."

"But I've got swimming soon," I said.

"Now!" said Brenda.

"Whoo, Stuart," said Eddie Mayhew. "You must be in trouble."

I didn't have the energy to be creatively rude; I just rolled my eyes and told him to shut up.

A few minutes later Brenda and I had settled ourselves under a secluded tree. We were sitting on my poncho, because the ground was still soaked from the rain the night before.

"Okay," said Brenda. "Give. I want to know what's going on around here. Did I have a nervous breakdown in the forest last night, or did I really see what I thought I saw?"

"You saw it, Toots," said Robert, shimmering into sight.

Brenda grabbed my arm. Her eyes grew big and round.

"Oh, poop," she said very softly.

Chapter Twelve

Why Ghosts Don't Use Libraries

"This isn't a joke, is it?" said Brenda nervously.

"Do you hear anyone laughing?" asked Robert.

Brenda scooted across the poncho in my direction; I could tell it was taking all her courage not to just get up and run. "Is he always like this?" she asked.

"No," I said. "Sometimes he's in a good mood. That's even worse."

"Oh," said Robert. "Must be everyone's in a bad mood this morning."

"What do you expect?" I yelled. Then I looked around to see if anyone had heard me "talking to myself" again. "What do you expect?" I said more softly. "After the stunt you pulled yesterday, you're lucky I'm still speaking to you."

Robert sighed. He turned toward Brenda. "The problem with Stuart," he said, "is that he never

understands when I'm doing him a favor. He'll remember last night as long as he lives. It'll be one
of the high points of his life. But does he say,
'Thank you, Robert'? Does he say, 'Wow, that was
neat, Robert'? No! All I get are complaints. And
then, when I break my own rule and reveal myself
to you, partly so you won't think he's crazy, does
he thank me? I repeat—No! No! and No!"

Robert crossed his arms and leaned against the
tree, looking sulky. I knew perfectly well it was
an act and that he was enjoying every minute of
it. But Brenda seemed impressed.

I decided to oblige him.

"Brenda Connors," I said, trying to sound formal,
"I'd like you to meet my friend, Robert Campbell.
Robert, my friend, Brenda."

"How do you do," said Robert graciously. "I'm
so pleased to make your acquaintance."

Brenda looked at me nervously. "Am I supposed
to shake hands with him?" she asked.

I shrugged. "It probably wouldn't work," I said.
"There's not much to him."

Robert raised one eyebrow. "That," he said, "was
a very low blow."

I shrugged. I figured he had it coming.

"How did you two meet?" asked Brenda. I could
see she was still having trouble with the fact that
she was actually talking to a ghost. I didn't blame

her; it had taken me awhile to get used to the idea, too.

Before I could answer her question, Robert launched into a long and complicated explanation of our first meeting. It was pretty funny, except for the fact that he was making most of it up.

"What *I* want to know is where you learned to make that potion," I said.

"That was easy," said Robert. "I just went back over to the Other Side and looked up the *real* Dr. Jekyll. He was so glad to have someone pay attention to him, he was more than willing to show me how to make his potion. It's one of the advantages of being a ghost. You get to meet the most interesting people."

Brenda was fascinated. "Who have you met?" she asked.

Robert shrugged. "Who haven't I met?" he said. "George Washington, Julius Caesar, Catherine the Great. I had tea with Queen Victoria and Genghis Khan once. It didn't go very well, though—his manners are terrible."

"Will you stop bragging!" I said. "And don't you encourage him," I added, turning to Brenda. I turned back to Robert. "What I want to know is how you put the potion there. You told me you can't move things around."

"I can't. At least, not without a lot of work."

67

"Hard work wouldn't kill you," I said sharply.

"That's true," said Robert. "You're getting very nasty, Stuart. Anyway, this is a slightly different process. I made up the potion on the Other Side and then transported it to this side. I just had to be sure to bring it to the right place, because I couldn't move it once I got it here."

"I'm more interested in that mummy," said Brenda. "I want to know how you made him appear."

"I didn't!" said Robert.

"Then what was it doing wandering around in the forest?" I said.

"I don't know," he replied. "I think it has something to do with you two. That's one of the reasons I'm bending my personal code and getting involved with two mortals at the same time. There's only room for one active dead man in this camp, and I'm it. I don't want that mummy on my turf."

"Well, what would a mummy want with us?" I asked.

"I did a little digging around last night while you two were sleeping." He snorted. "Sleep—what a waste of time! Anyway, another advantage of being a ghost is that you don't have to use the library; you can go straight to the source. Well, I didn't ask the mummy—you can't understand a word it says with all those bandages on its face. But I did talk to a couple of old Egyptians I know and they told me if a mummy is wandering around, it probably means someone stole something that belongs to it. And he wants it back."

"The thing the deliverymen took!" I cried.

"I hope you don't consider that a brilliant insight," said Robert.

"What thing?" asked Brenda. "What deliverymen?"

I told her what Robert had seen the day the mummy arrived at camp.

"Well, then the mummy should be after the deliverymen," she said, "not us."

"Maybe it just happened to run into us while it was wandering around looking for—for whatever it is it's looking for."

"I don't think so," said Brenda. "It really looked as if it was coming after us." She hesitated, then said, "I think it's been after me before. Remember when I told you about those weird noises I heard outside our bunk that night? Well, the next morning when I went outside, I got a whiff of that horrible odor we smelled last night."

"But why would the mummy be after you?" I asked.

And then it all clicked into place. "That gold bug with the stone!" I yelled. "I knew it looked familiar. It's not something from the prop shop.

It's a scarab—an Egyptian scarab. It must belong to the mummy."

"But how did it end up beside the path?" asked Brenda. "Someone who stole a thing like that wouldn't just drop it in the bushes."

"He would if he was scared enough," said Robert. He sounded embarrassed. I looked at him. If he were alive, he would have been blushing.

"What do you mean?" I asked.

He sighed. "I didn't want to tell you, because I didn't want you to know I had exposed myself to someone else. Generally, I'm not that kind of ghost. But I did try to scare those guys after they stole the thing from the mummy case. They ran like crazy. I didn't see them drop anything, but who knows—maybe the scarab fell out of one of their pockets while they were running."

"Then that thing is real gold?" said Brenda in shock. "Good grief, I just threw it in my trunk."

"Well, you've got to give it back, or you'll have that mummy chasing you all over the place," said Robert.

"I'll give it to Mr. Stevens this morning," she said.

"No good," I answered. "Mr. Stevens is in Hollywood right now."

"Then I'll give it to Peter Flinches," she said.

"That's no good either," said Robert. "Flinches

won't give it back to the mummy. He'll keep it for Stevens. And when he gives it to Stevens, that doesn't mean it will go back to the mummy. Which means the mummy is going to keep looking for it. And since you're the last one who had it . . ."

Robert trailed off to let us figure things out for ourselves.

Chapter Thirteen

The Un-Burglars

"So what do we do?" asked Brenda nervously.

Robert shrugged. "I think you'd better sneak into the Cottage and give that scarab back to the mummy."

"I don't even want to think about this," I said. I stood up. "I'm late for swimming."

"Stuart!" cried Brenda as I started to walk away. "You can't leave me here with him!"

"You're safe," I said. "He doesn't bite."

"No, but I bark," said Robert.

I kept walking.

As you can imagine, despite what I said, I *did* think about this mess—a lot, which got me in trouble during swimming.

"Stuart," said Splash when I crashed into the dock for the second time, "are you going to swim or daydream?"

I wish daydreaming was all it was. As far as I

was concerned, my thoughts were definitely in the nightmare category.

All morning I continued to think about returning the scarab. Finally I decided that Robert was right. We did have to return the scarab.

"I have to talk to you."

Brenda and I said those words simultaneously when we met at the door of the dining hall for lunch.

"Good," we said, still talking together. We laughed, which pleased me, since I suspected it would be awhile before I found anything very amusing again.

After we had eaten, we met at the spot where we had talked with Robert earlier.

"Boy, was I mad at you this morning," said Brenda. "When you walked off and left me with that ghost, I decided I'd never speak to you again as long as I live. But after a while I decided it was okay. He's a real sweetie-pie."

"Robert?" I said. "A sweetie-pie?"

Brenda ignored my tone of voice. "Anyway, he gave me a message for you. He said there's a big bottle of the Dr. Jekyll potion in your trunk anytime you want to use it."

"Why in heaven's name would I want to use that stuff?" I said. "Hasn't it caused enough trouble already?"

Suddenly I felt a tight little knot of fear in my midsection. Had I remembered to lock my trunk that morning? What if Lucius went rummaging through it, the way he had the night he painted my underwear?

I shook my head. I must have locked it. After the underwear episode, I had vowed to be very careful about that.

"I didn't say you *would* want to use the potion," said Brenda, interrupting my thoughts. "I'm just giving you the message. If it was mine, I'd go back and pour it out as soon as possible. Now what did you want to talk to me about?"

"I'll go with you," I said.

"I beg your pardon?"

"I'll go with you—to take the scarab back to the mummy."

"Oh, I knew that," said Brenda. "What time shall we meet?"

I started to ask how she knew I had decided to go, but I figured it wasn't worth the effort. I decided when I got home I'd ask my father if it was always this way with women.

We decided to meet at midnight; that was the earliest we figured we could get out after bunk check.

Knowing what was coming, I expected the rest of the day to drag. But there was so much going

74

on, I hardly had time to worry. First Harry canceled filming, but he wanted me to help him with some special effects. Then Splash called me back for a little extra practice for the meet. Then we had a meeting of the panel members for the special showing of *Cry of the Sasquatch*, which was the next night. Before I knew it, Dan was calling, "Lights out." I was exhausted, and I hadn't had time to do even half the worrying I had been planning on.

Now the main thing I was worried about was whether or not I'd be able to stay awake until it was time to meet Brenda.

Fortunately (I guess) I had Robert to act as a living (sort of) alarm clock.

"Sto-o-o-o-art," he whispered in my ear a couple of hours later. "Time to get u-u-u-up."

I sat up straight in my bed. The room was pitch-dark. I could hear the slow, steady breathing of the other guys around me.

What time was it? Had I missed my meeting with Brenda?

Digging under my pillow, I found my watch. The faint glow of the lines and numbers told me I had eleven minutes to slip out of bed, get dressed, and walk over to the trail to meet Brenda.

"Come on!" said Robert as I was slipping on my sweatshirt. "Let's make tracks!"

I love it. He can bug me with no one hearing him; but if I try to answer back, I'm bound to wake someone up. What a system!

"I thought you'd never get here," said Brenda when I trotted up to her on the path. I looked at my watch—I was one minute late. What was this, Let's-Dump-On-Stuart-Night?

"Have you got the scarab?" I asked, ignoring her complaint.

"Right here," she said, patting her pocket.

I glanced up the hill. "Well, let's get going," I said.

She nodded.

But neither of us started to move. I figured Brenda was thinking the same thing I was thinking: what were we going to do when we got up there? Even if we could get inside and make it to the mummy room without getting caught—what then? Should we just drop the scarab at the base of the case? Or would that leave the possibility that someone might come in and pick it up before the mummy could get it? Should we open the case and put the scarab back inside?

The thought painted an unhappy picture in my head. In my imagination I saw myself opening the case and finding myself face to face with an angry mummy, who reached up with his powerful arms and began to drag me into the case with him.

Of course, it was entirely possible the mummy was out wandering around, looking for us or, more specifically, for Brenda.

I swallowed.

"Well," said Brenda, looking up the trail.

"Well," I answered, nodding.

"Oh, for the love of pete, shut up and move!" said Robert in exasperation.

Brenda and I looked at each other nervously, then started up the path.

Chapter Fourteen

Inside the Cottage

The Cottage stood at the top of a hill that rose from the shores of Misty Lake. The lake was living up to its name that night; a shifting cloud of white mist swirled above the water. Long tendrils of fog groped upward along the moonbeams.

From the outside, Gregory Steven's new house didn't look that much different from most of the summer homes that belonged to the rich people who lived on the opposite shore of the lake where my family had vacationed the summer before. It *was* bigger than a typical cottage. But if what Robert had told me was true, what I was seeing now was only a small part of what lay within. We stood just inside the line of the trees and stared at it.

"Is there anyone staying here while Mr. Stevens is out of town?" Brenda asked softly.

"I don't know," I said. According to some rumors, the Cottage was protected electronically; other people had told me it was staffed by full-time security guards—anywhere from one to fifteen, depending on who you relied on for your gossip; still others claimed that Gregory Stevens had built out here because he didn't want a lot of elaborate security devices. He was counting on our respect for him to keep us out of his new home.

I felt bad about breaking in. But I reminded myself that we weren't there to steal anything. We were trying to *unsteal* something.

"Any advice?" I asked Robert.

That ghost may be a pain, but in situations like this he's great. Sometimes there's a definite advantage to having a friend who can turn invisible and walk through walls!

"Just a minute," he said. Then he vanished. Brenda, who still hadn't had time to get used to Robert's abrupt arrivals and departures, let out a little cry of surprise.

"Shhhh!" I hissed.

We waited.

After a few minutes Robert reappeared. "As far as I can tell, there's no one inside," he said. "The front door has a special lock. But—"

Here he paused and favored us with a grin so smug I thought I would be sick.

He continued, ''It just so happens that I was watching when the deliverymen came in, and I know how to operate the lock.''

I suppose I should have been pleased. But secretly I had hoped that we wouldn't be able to get in, so that we would have to go back. I looked at Brenda. She nodded grimly as we followed Robert up the steps.

The door was made of dark wood, polished so carefully that it glowed in the moonlight. Mounted on the jamb to the right of the door was a keypad, identical to the kind you find on a Touch-tone phone.

Robert closed his eyes and recited a number. I punched the buttons as he spoke. As I touched the fourth button the door swung slowly open. Music began to play—low, spooky music.

''You may now enter,'' whispered a hoarse voice.

''It's just tricks,'' I said. ''Mechanical tricks.'' But whether I was trying to reassure Brenda or myself I couldn't tell.

We stepped through the door into a dark hallway, Robert floating beside us. Suddenly Brenda grabbed my arm. ''Stuart!'' she gasped. I looked in the direction she was pointing and nearly fainted.

Frankenstein's monster had just walked around the corner. For a minute I thought I was going to die. My heart was pounding so hard that if I could

have connected it to a generator I would have supplied electricity to the entire camp.

The creature shambled forward. Its green face glowed in the dark. I could see the bolts in its neck.

"Who dares intrude on this house?" it moaned.

Suddenly I remembered where we were. "Come on," I said. I grabbed Brenda by the arm and marched forward.

"Stuart!" she hissed. "What are you doing!"

"Stand back!" said the creature. "Beware my wrath."

Then it dissolved into nothingness as we walked through the spot where it had been standing.

Brenda sighed. "It was just one of those things that Harry makes," she said in relief.

"A holographic projection," I said.

"That's what Stuart thought I was when he first met me," said Robert. He sounded offended.

"But how did you know this thing wasn't real?" asked Brenda.

"How could it be?" I asked.

"Well, Robert and the mummy aren't holograms. So how did you know this was?"

"Because it looked like Boris Karloff."

"So?"

"So he played the monster in the movies, back in the 1930s. It's just the movie version, not the real thing. So it couldn't possibly be real."

Brenda looked at me as if I were out of my mind.

"Trust me," I said. "Monsters are my specialty."

We started to move forward again.

"Do you want some light?" asked Robert. "I know where the switches are."

I shook my head; no sense in drawing attention to ourselves. I figured our flashlight should be enough. Of course, I was dying to look around. But I was also terrified of getting caught. I would be happy if we could just give the scarab back to the mummy and get out in one piece.

We walked down a long hall.

"This way," said Robert, pointing to a big wooden door. I noticed that he was whispering. I wondered if he was nervous, too.

"Where does this lead?" I asked.

"Downstairs—to the main part of the house."

I nodded and turned the handle. Suddenly a siren began to whoop. Bells clanged. Buzzers began blatting so loudly they made my teeth vibrate.

We ran.

Chapter Fifteen

The Jerk with
the Jekyll Juice

Brenda and I huddled under a bush at the bottom of the hill, watching nervously as counselors and staff members ran around, shining their flashlights in all directions. I was terrified—even more frightened than when we had seen the mummy in the woods. What would happen if they found us? Could we get anyone to believe our story? Or would we be thrown out of camp, maybe even be arrested?

Fortunately, ghosts make great lookouts. Since no one else could see Robert, it was easy for him to stand right in the open, look around, and then gesture to us when the coast was clear. With his help we got away without anyone seeing us.

But our mission had been a failure. We were no further ahead than we had been when we started.

The mummy still didn't have his scarab, and Brenda still wasn't safe from him.

Of course, there was always a chance that if he came after her, she could just toss him the scarab and he'd turn and go away.

But would you want to bet your life on a mummy's good humor?

When I got back to Bunk Thirteen I found that most of the other kids had been roused by all the noise. I wandered in, yawning and stretching, pretending that I had just gone out to the latrine for a litte while.

"What's going on?" asked Eddie Mayhew.

"You got me," I said, faking another yawn. "I sat down in the outhouse and all of a sudden bells and whistles started going off. For a minute I thought I'd won a prize."

Eddie laughed, and I slipped back into my bunk.

I was just drifting off when I opened my eyes wide and stared into the darkness. I had been so busy, I'd completely forgotten Brenda's message about Robert's placing a big supply of the monster potion in my trunk.

I couldn't sleep, worrying about it. Finally I crawled out of my bunk. I had to get rid of that stuff fast—before we had another problem. Trying not to make any noise, I opened the trunk and began rummaging through it. But I couldn't find any sign of the potion. My stomach began thinking up new kinds of knots to tie itself into. Had Robert just been joking?

Or had someone gone through my trunk and found the stuff?

Had I really been dumb enough to leave the thing unlocked again?

"Oh, I put it there all right," said Robert when I confronted him later that morning.

"Why would you do a thing like that?" I asked angrily.

"I thought you might like it," he said. He was so genuinely surprised that I was mad, I didn't have the heart to stay angry with him.

"Look, you've got to make me up a batch of the antidote," I said. "Just in case something happens."

"If you insist," said Robert. He slowly wavered out of sight. When he was completely gone, I heard a voice from the empty air say, "I'll get right on it."

More special effects!

Even though I had my suspicions, it wasn't until that night that I finally knew who had taken the potion.

That night, you'll remember, was our big night—the world premiere of *Cry of the Sasquatch*, combined with the official opening of the Camp

86

Haunted Hills Movie Palace. We had already shown a rough cut of the film. But this was a more polished version, complete with sound effects and music. Mr. Stevens had even brought in some of his Hollywood buddies for the event. People in camp were so excited that it was dangerous to touch anyone. You had the feeling that if contact was made, they might up and explode.

Even though everyone had known about the big event for days, we all found official invitations beside our plates at breakfast that morning. Since they were trying to make this evening seem as special as possible, the staff had decided to have a bug juice and Fritos reception after the film and panel discussion. In the best Camp Haunted Hills fashion, the whole thing was scheduled to start at midnight.

Even though I had gotten used to the idea of being on the panel that was going to discuss the making of the film, I was still kind of nervous; after all, I'd never done anything like that before. So I went over to the building a little early. I thought it might make me more comfortable to see how things had been set up, where I was going to be sitting—stuff like that.

Even though we called it the Movie Palace, the new theater was really a multipurpose building; it had been designed so that it could be used for plays, and big meetings, and other things like that. But it also had state-of-the-art projection and sound equipment, and some of the most comfortable chairs I have ever personally sat in.

If that sounds like a lot for a summer camp, remember who put this place together. People say no one has ever loved movies as much as Gregory Stevens does. They also say that no one has ever made as much money on them as Mr. Stevens has. So if he wants a fancy theater for his camp, you can believe he's going to *have* a fancy theater for his camp.

Anyway, when I got to the Palace I slipped in the back way and sat halfway down the auditorium. I could hear noise from the kitchen downstairs, where the cook was getting the snacks ready.

The house lights were down. In the dim glow from the safety lights I could see the table up on the stage, where the panel was going to sit. Six places had been set up at the table. Each place had a name tag, a microphone, a pitcher, and a water glass.

My name tag was at the far right side.

Standing next to it, pouring something into my water pitcher, was Lucius Colton.

All of a sudden I knew what had happened to the Jekyll juice. I must have left my trunk unlocked again. When Lucius had gone poking around in it to see what kind of trouble he could cause, he must have found the bottle of Jekyll juice, put two and two together, and figured out what had happened to him on Wednesday. He'd probably also decided it had been all my fault—and that he was going to pay me back.

So this was going to be my reward for risking my life to get the antidote to him that night in the woods: a chance to be a monster, myself!

Chapter Sixteen

Recipe for a Disaster

Lucius didn't realize I was in the room. He went slinking down the steps of the stage and along the side of the theater. I slipped out of my seat and followed him. This time the creep had gone too far. This time I was going to have it out with him.

We were at the rear of the theater, where the cook had set up the refreshment tables, when I spoke to him.

"Nice stunt, Lucius," I said quietly. It did my heart good to see the way Lucius jumped when he heard my voice. "Even if you really did have a reason to want to get back at me—which you don't—did you think about what might happen to the rest of the people here if you turn me into a monster? Or don't you care?"

"Well, if it isn't my old friend, Stuart," he said, his voice smooth as cream—or grease. "What's the matter, Stuart?" he purred. "Don't you like the little surprise I was fixing up for you? I wouldn't worry about the others in the room. You're such a stupid little goody-goody that when we let out the monster side of your personality you'll probably just grow a mustache and have a couple of teeth get snaggly. We'll all have a good laugh, and no one will be in any danger at all."

"Do you really believe that?" I asked, trying to sound dangerous.

Lucius just laughed.

"Look," I said, "what's this all about, anyway? I never did anything to you. But from the moment I met you, you've done nothing but tease me and pick on me. You've been totally rotten to me, and I don't even know why."

I don't know what I expected from this little speech. If I thought it was going to create some kind of bond of honesty with Lucius—that he was suddenly going to start crying and tell me about some horrible incident in his childhood that had warped his personality, and then beg my forgiveness for all he had done to me—I had another think coming. This was real life, not the movies. He just looked at me and said, "I don't like your face, Glassman. I never have, not from the first time I saw you."

How's that for a deep and penetrating analysis of our problem?

91

I lost my temper and brought my magnificent vocabulary into play. "You creep!" I said.

"Come on, Glassman," he said. He set the bottle of potion on the table and wiggled his fingers at me. "Come here. Try it. I've been dying for you to take a swing at me."

Something snapped inside me, and I charged him. He grabbed me. I grabbed back. As we struggled, we bumped into the table. Suddenly I heard a loud splash.

I looked at the table. The potion was gone.

"Lucius," I said. "The potion. We've got to—"

He didn't pay any attention. He was trying to wrestle me to the floor. I figured if he succeeded, the next step would be to start pounding my face.

"Lucius, the—"

"Shut up, Glassman," he said. "I've had enough of you."

And then the adrenaline hit.

"Lucius!" I roared. *"Bug off!"* With that I broke his grip, grabbed him by the arms, and pushed him away from me so hard that he ran into the wall.

Naturally, he started to cry.

I guess I am a goody-goody. Even though I was totally disgusted, if I hadn't had other things on my mind, I probably would have gone over to see if he was all right. "And you'd probably have gotten punched in the face for your trouble," noted Robert

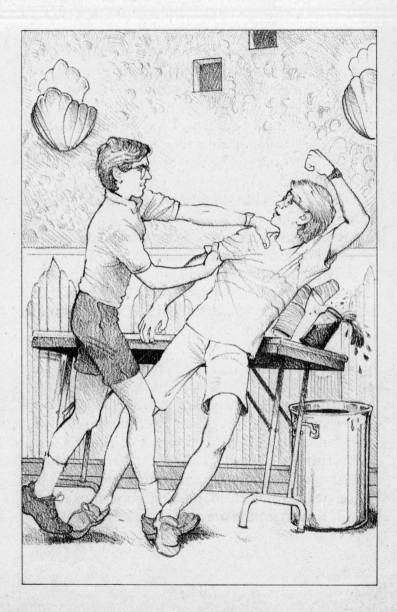

when I was discussing the matter with him later.

Well, Robert and I have different philosophies of life (or death, or whatever it is a ghost has a philosophy of).

Anyway, at the moment, I was far more worried about what had happened to that potion than about Lucius. Fortunately, he decided to remove himself from the situation.

"I hate you, Glassman!" he screamed. Then he ran out of the room.

Sigh. I still don't know what I did to deserve all that. I decided to think about it later. First things first, which in this case meant the potion.

It didn't take me long to find it. If you think about what kind of week I had had so far, you can probably guess where it was.

That's right. The bottle had fallen into the big vat of bug juice the cook had prepared to serve after the movie.

At first I couldn't figure out why it wasn't bubbling and streaming. Then I remembered—that part had always been some trick of Harry's. Robert's stuff had no special effects to warn people off. It just sat there, mixed into a huge vat of red bug juice, waiting to turn the first poor sucker who drank it into a monster.

Chapter Seventeen

Toast—and a Jam

I decided to dump the stuff outside. I tried to pick up the vat, but it was too heavy for me. I was trying to figure out how to dump it inside without ruining the carpet, when the mess hall director, who was also in charge of the reception, walked in.

"Hey, Stuart," he said, "that's for later. Get out of here now, and wait your turn like everyone else."

I decided to approach the problem in a grown-up manner. "You shouldn't serve that bug juice tonight," I said, trying to sound serious.

He laughed. "Kids have said that at every camp I've ever worked at," he said. "I suppose you want Canada Dry instead. Forget it. Now scram!"

"But—"

"Get out of here, kid."

The man had arms like telephone poles. Blue

dragon tattoos coiled around his wrists. He was holding a big metal spoon, and when he raised it and started to shake it at me, I decided the discussion was over.

As I was heading out the back door I saw the first campers lining up to come in the front way.

A disaster was in the making, and I didn't have much time to stop it. Running as fast as I could, I raced back to the bunk and dug around in my trunk, hoping that Robert had made up some more antidote as he had promised. He had! That guy does come through sometimes. I had no idea what I was going to do with it. But I decided it was better to have it than not.

I ran back to the theater, getting there just in time to join the others on the panel in the Green Room—the room people waited in before going on stage.

I had the antidote, but I still couldn't figure out what to do with it. I considered trying to mix it with the punch. But waiters were standing guard over the refreshment table to keep kids from eating everything ahead of schedule. Besides, I didn't know what would happen if I mixed the two potions together: would they cancel each other out, or create something even worse? For all I knew, they might explode. I could just see the headlines: "HOLLYWOOD'S MOST SUCCESSFUL DIRECTOR KILLED

BY EXPLODING BUG JUICE: Frightened Camper Held For Questioning. Pictures on Page 11."

Finally I just hid the antidote backstage, figuring that at least it would be there if it was needed. I still planned on stopping anyone from drinking the potion.

It was time for things to get started. I don't know how the discussion went, because I was so worried about what was going to happen after the film that I hardly paid attention to a word of it. I couldn't keep my eyes off the punch bowl, which was now filled to the brim with Jekyll juice.

After the discussion, we took seats in the second row of the auditorium. The film went beautifully. Harry had brought over the mist machine, and before the film began, someone behind the screen pumped the theater full of fog. It was really neat— especially when they started the projector and you could actually see the picture right on the mist.

After that it was time for the reception. I turned around and looked back at the table. During the film someone had been ladling the juice into glasses. It was all ready to drink!

Well, what's the worst that can happen? I asked myself, trying to look on the bright side. Someone would drink the stuff, turn into a monster, and we'd have another incident. Maybe even two or three people would get transformed. I'd get them

97

to take the antidote and then no one else would drink the stuff. It wouldn't be all *that* bad.

That was when Gregory Stevens himself walked onstage and said that he wanted everyone to drink a toast to the filmmakers. The waiters started walking down the aisles of the theater, handing out glasses of punch.

I couldn't believe it. They were all going to drink the stuff at once!

"Excuse me," I whispered to the others in my row. "Excuse me, I've got to go to the bathroom!"

"You can't go now," whispered Harry. "They're going to drink the toast!"

I screwed my face into what I hoped was a grimace of pain. "I think I'm going to throw up," I said.

"Go!" said Harry.

Brenda was sitting at the end of the row. I grabbed her by the arm as I went past. "Come with me," I said.

I didn't know what I was going to do. I couldn't stand up and yell, "Don't drink that stuff!" They'd send for the men in the white coats. I did know I couldn't be in that room when that toast was drunk.

"Stuart!" Brenda said angrily as I half dragged her out of her seat. "What are you doing?"

"Just come with me!" I insisted.

We got as far as the doorway. Then I couldn't resist. I turned back to look. Mr. Stevens was just finishing the toast.

"So let's all raise our cups and drink to the career of a brilliant new director—Harry Housen!"

Everyone began to cheer. Then they lifted their cups and drank the toast.

Five seconds later all hell broke loose as everyone in the room started growing furry hands and faces. We slammed the door. Brenda looked at me in horror.

"Did you do that?" she whispered.

"Well, sort of," I said. "But it wasn't really my fault."

"Stuart!"

I could hear a lecture coming. "Never mind that now," I snapped. "We've got to figure out some way to get them to take the antidote!"

"You must be kidding!" said Brenda. "Listen to that."

She paused so I could hear the hubbub on the other side of the door. It sounded like a full-scale riot.

"Can't you hear how they're rampaging around in there?" she said. "How are you going to get all those people to drink that stuff? About the only way we could get it down them is to make them breathe it."

99

Sometimes I'm brilliant, even if it is by accident. Or maybe I'm only half-brilliant. After all, it was Brenda who had just given me the idea.

"Come on," I said. "I think I know what to do."

I grabbed her by the hand and started running down the hall.

Chapter Eighteen

Monsters in the Mist

Without taking time to explain, I dragged Brenda to the area behind the screen.

The shouts and snarls from inside the theater were getting worse. When we reached the back-stage area, we were greeted by a truly terrifying sight. Because the screen was translucent and the lights in the theater were on high, we could see everything that was happening on the other side, as if it were a shadow play.

And what was happening was appalling. Kids and adults were shouting and fighting, jumping over chairs, and chasing one another. The sounds were even worse—a constantly increasing mix of howls and screams, snorts and growls.

It was anyone's guess what might happen if we didn't do something fast.

"Open the mist machine," I said, running to where I had hidden the antidote.

Brenda was still struggling with the top of the machine when I got back. I realized she had never used it before.

"Here," I said, handing her the bottle of antidote. "You uncork this—I'll take care of the machine."

All this took only a few seconds. But they were the longest seconds I ever lived through. Finally, I lifted the cover to the mist compartment so that Brenda could pour the antidote into the machine. My fingers were trembling as I screwed the top back in place.

"Okay, poke the hose around the corner of the screen," I said. "Be careful—if you attract their attention, they'll be all over us before you know it."

I figured the only good thing about what was going on out there was that no one had an unfair advantage: they were *all* monsters.

Brenda took the hose and tucked it under the screen. But before I could start pumping, someone grabbed my arms from behind.

"Well, well, well," said a nasty voice that was all too familiar. "So you're all set to play the hero again, huh, Glassman? I've got a better idea. Why don't we just let things roll for a bit."

"Lucius—"

He tightened his grip on my arms. "Shut up and listen, Stuart. See, I've got this all worked out. I figure once people start to put things together, they're going to realize that this is all your fault."

I squirmed. I had to get at the mist machine. But Lucius had my arms pinned tight. I couldn't believe he thought that getting revenge was more important than getting everyone turned back to normal as soon as possible.

"After all," he continued calmly, "who was it who had the antidote when this happened to me? Everyone else thought it was a joke then. But now that they know it's for real, they're going to start thinking about who caused it. I'm interested to see just how much trouble you'll end up in. My guess is they'll pack you off to reform school."

"Lucius, you can't be serious," said Brenda. She had to yell to be heard above the howling in the theater. "I'll tell everyone what really happened."

"They won't believe you, stupid," said Lucius smugly. "It's obvious you're his accomplice. After all, you're the only other ones besides me who didn't get turned into monsters tonight." He snickered. "And no one is going to know that the only reason I didn't turn into a monster is because I knew better than to drink that stuff. I'm going to tell them it's because you two already did this to me once, so I was immune when I drank the toast."

The noise on the other side of the screen was deafening.

"I'll let you go in a second, Stuart. Then *I'll* pump the machine—though I suppose you can fight me for it if you want. It doesn't really matter who does it. As long as I'm here when everyone changes back, my story is going to work better than yours."

I slumped in his arms. I wondered if he really hated me enough to lie like this.

Something told me he did.

I was just imagining myself being hauled off to jail when Robert showed up. He didn't bother to reveal himself to Lucius. He didn't need to. It was enough for Lucius to see who Robert had brought with him—the mummy.

It raised its arms and started shambling toward us.

"Don't be scared," said Robert cheerfully. "That's just the way he walks. If you'll just give him the scarab, he'll be glad to leave you alone."

A puzzled look crossed his face. "What's making all that noise?" he asked.

Part of what was making the noise was Lucius. He had taken one look at the monstrous mummy shambling toward us, screamed, and run in the opposite direction.

I always suspected he was a coward at heart.

While Brenda timidly handed the scarab to the mummy, I fell on the machine and started pumping for all I was worth, all the time praying that there would be enough antidote to go around—and that my strength would hold out.

The mist machine hissed as I sent the antidote pouring into the theater.

"Keep pumping!" cried Brenda. "Keep pumping!"

But the machine was empty. I joined her at the edge of the screen and peeked into the theater. It was filled with clouds of thick white mist. I could see dark forms leaping and pouncing through the fog.

"Nice work," said Robert, floating up behind us. "Too bad you don't have a camera here."

"You've been hanging around film people too long," I said.

Suddenly the mist began to take effect. Within seconds the hubbub started to die down. And as the mist began to clear, I saw that the monsters were gone—replaced by a group of very groggy, very confused campers, counselors, and Hollywood big-shots.

Well, the rest, as they say, is history. There were some pretty angry people, of course. But no one knew who to blame—especially since everyone's memory of the whole affair was so dim. They all knew they had bruises, aching muscles, and torn clothes. But they couldn't quite remember how they'd gotten them. And even if they did, the whole thing was so unbelievable, it would have been hard to take action against anyone. I think, in the end, everyone just decided to pretend it had been a bad dream.

But the last time I talked to Harry Housen about what happened that day, he got a gleam in his eye and this kind of faraway look that I've learned to recognize as genius in action.

So don't be surprised if you see a movie something like this, sometime in the next few years.

If you do, just remember—you read it here first!

About the Author and Illustrator

Bruce Coville has written over a dozen books for young readers, including *Sarah's Unicorn* and *The Monster's Ring.* He has also written three musical plays for young audiences. Mr. Coville was born in the central New York area where he has lived most of his life. Before becoming a full-time writer, he worked as a magazine editor, a teacher, a toymaker, and a gravedigger. He is the author of the first Camp Haunted Hills book, *How I Survived My Summer Vacation.*

Tom Newsom was born in Texas and has been a freelance artist since his graduation from Art Center College. He has done many book covers for young readers, and his illustrations have appeared in such magazines as *Discover, Reader's Digest,* and *Field & Stream.*